GALAXY ZACK

Game Over, Nebulon

By Ray O'Ryan

Illustrated by Jason Kraft

LITTLE SIMON
New York London Toronto Sydney New Delhi

This book is a work of fiction. Any references to historical events, real people, or real places are used fictitiously. Other names, characters, places, and events are products of the author's imagination, and any resemblance to actual events or places or persons, living or dead, is entirely coincidental.

LITTLE SIMON
An imprint of Simon & Schuster Children's Publishing Division
1230 Avenue of the Americas, New York, New York 10020
First Little Simon paperback edition December 2022
 For information about special discounts for bulk purchases, please contact Simon & Schuster Special Sales at 1-866-506-1949 or business@simonandschuster.com.
The Simon & Schuster Speakers Bureau can bring authors to your live event. For more information or to book an event contact the Simon & Schuster Speakers Bureau at 1-866-248-3049 or visit our website at www.simonspeakers.com.
Designed by Claire Torres
1022 LAK
1 2 3 4 5 6 7 8 9 10 This book has been cataloged with the Library of Congress.
978-1-6659-1926-5 (hc)
978-1-6659-1925-8 (pbk)
978-1-6659-1927-2 (ebook)

CONTENTS

Chapter 1
The Intergalactic Games

Zack Nelson listened carefully as his teacher, Ms. Rudolph, began her lesson on planets. It was one of Zack's favorite subjects. Ever since his family moved from Earth to Nebulon, Zack loved learning about the galaxy and planet-hopping to brand-new places.

While Ms. Rudolph was talking about the ten rings of Circulus, Zack looked around the room. Everyone was busy whispering about something.

"Hey, Drake," Zack said to his best friend. "Why is everyone so excited?"

Drake leaned over with a huge smile on his face. "Do you not remember? The Intergalactic Games are this weekend!"

"Oh, of course!" Zack said. He had been looking forward to it all week. That *was* exciting news!

Right then Ms. Rudolph stopped and cleared her throat. "We'll end the lesson here today because I have an exciting announcement to make," she began.

Zack and Drake and their friend Seth Stevens sat up straighter in their seats.

"As you all know, the Intergalactic Games are this weekend. The Games are a galaxy-wide competition that happens when neighboring planets align with each other," Ms. Rudolph explained. "When this cosmic shift occurs, visitors from all over the galaxy are invited to a new host planet!"

The entire class cheered excitedly. Spots to participate in the Games were limited this year. Zack and his friends had entered a student lottery and were waiting to hear the results.

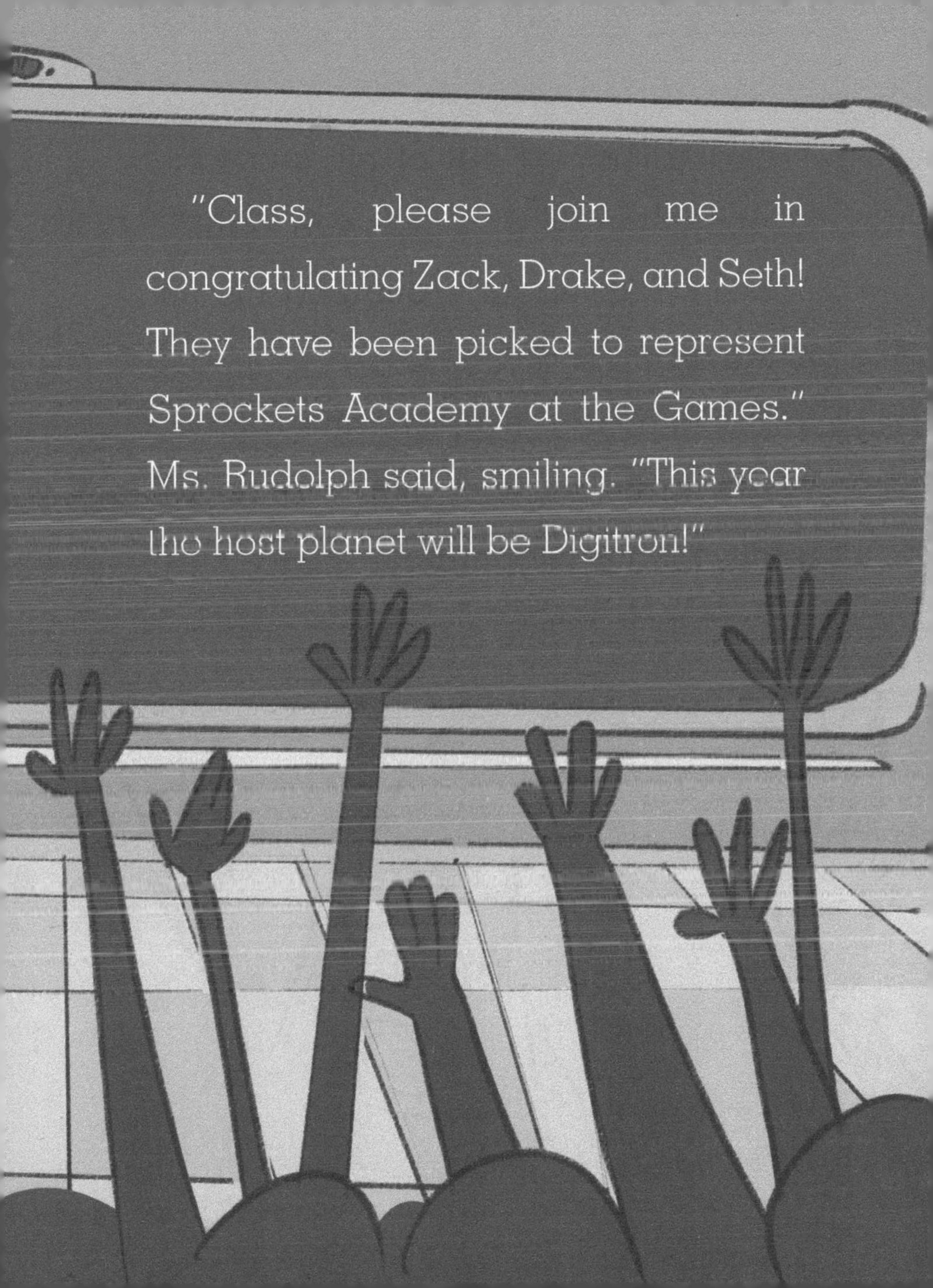

"Class, please join me in congratulating Zack, Drake, and Seth! They have been picked to represent Sprockets Academy at the Games." Ms. Rudolph said, smiling. "This year the host planet will be Digitron!"

Drake jumped out of his seat and happily shouted, "Yippee-wah-wah!"

Even Seth eagerly pumped his fist in the air.

Digitron was a video game planet, where real everyday life and virtual reality blended together.

Wow, Zack thought. *Could there be anything cooler than living inside a video game world?*

Zack and his friends had visited all kinds of awesome planets before, but he couldn't wait to see what Digitron was like. A video game planet sounded like the grapest place in the galaxy!

Chapter 2

Digitron Days

As soon as he got home, Zack zoomed into the elevator and headed straight to his bedroom to start packing for his trip.

"Hey, Ira!" Zack called to the Nelson family's Indoor Robotic Assistant.

"Welcome home, Master Just Zack. How may I assist you?" Ira replied.

"I need to pack for my trip to Digitron. I'm going to compete in the Intergalactic Games!" Zack cheered. "Can you help me?"

"Of course, Master Just Zack," said Ira.

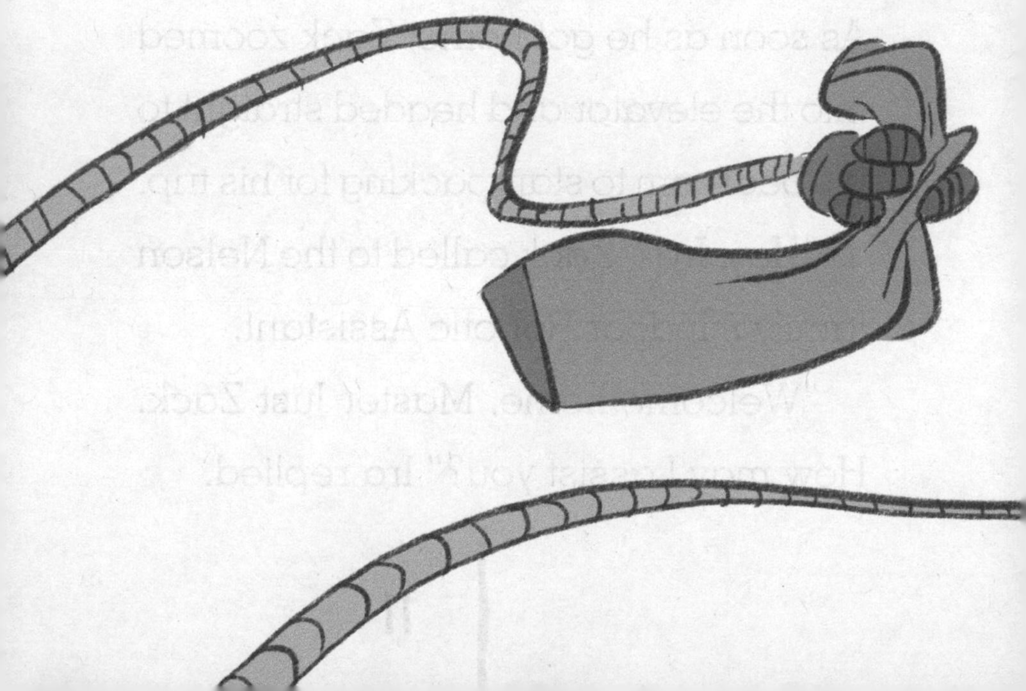

A panel in the ceiling opened, and a pair of extendable robot arms holding a travel space case dangled down. Zack watched in awe as Ira swiftly folded and packed a bunch of clothes into his travel space case.

Right as Ira finished, Zack's mom called him down for dinner. So he quickly jumped back into the elevator to go to the kitchen.

"Ira, could we please have some galactic patties and crispy fritters?" Mrs. Nelson said, when everyone was seated.

"Of course. Coming right up," Ira replied. Then a ceiling panel slid open, and five galactic patties and crispy fritters appeared.

"Thank you, Ira!" the family said at the same time.

"Mmm, yumzers," Zack said happily as he chewed a big mouthful.

"So, Captain, are you excited for your big trip?" Zack's dad asked.

"You bet I am," Zack replied.

"Do you know what Digitron will be like?" Mr. Nelson asked.

"Ummm, not really," Zack mumbled.

He realized that he had been so focused on the idea of playing life-size video games, battling virtual space monsters, and flying through grape galaxy obstacles that he hadn't given any thought to how it actually worked.

"Why don't we ask Ira to set up a little 'presentation' for us while we eat?" Mr. Nelson continued. "Ira?"

"Yes, Master Otto," Ira responded.

"Show us what life on Digitron looks like," Mr. Nelson said.

Ira dimmed the lights, and suddenly a holographic image beamed into the middle of the dining room. Ira then began to explain how Digitron had two dimensions—an everyday life dimension and a virtual reality dimension. On the everyday life dimension, life was pretty normal. But on the virtual reality gaming dimension, Digitronians could live inside different video games!

Zack was surprised to see that even on a planet like Digitron, kids went to school, ate dinner, and played sports—just like Zack and his friends did.

But going into the Digitron gaming portal looked *nothing* like regular life. Suddenly the Nelsons' dining table sprouted pixel buildings, pixel trees, and pixel sidewalks!

"Once you are inside the gaming portal, you are able to enter into a virtual gaming dimension, where players live

inside the game," Ira explained. "And you, Master Just Zack, and your friends, Drake Taylor and Seth Stevens, shall be the first kids from Nebulon to play these games."

"Yippee-wah-wah!" he hooted when Ira finished the presentation. "This is going to be so grape!"

The next morning, after a yummy breakfast of nebu-cakes, Zack and his family piled into their flying car and headed to the Creston City Spaceport, where they met Ms. Rudolph, Drake and Seth, and their families.

"Students, our ship is ready to go," Ms. Rudolph told the boys.

Zack, Drake, and Seth each turned to their families to say goodbye.

"Mom, Dad, I promise to do my best to make you and all of Nebulon proud of us," Zack said.

He could hear his friends making similar pledges to their own families.

Zack threw his arms around his parents and even hugged his twin sisters, Charlotte and Cathy. Then he picked up his space case and was ready to go.

Chapter 3

Up, Up, and Away!

Ms. Rudolph led the three boys onto the space cruiser and helped them find their seats. Once he was settled, Zack pressed his face against the window.

"There is nothing cooler than cruising through space—except maybe being inside a video game!" Drake piped up.

"Absolutely!" Zack agreed.

"Look, nebu-nuts," Seth said, as a panel on the wall of the space cruiser opened to reveal a box of snacks.

"And spudsy melonade!" Drake added. Another panel opened, and three cups of the juicy drink appeared.

"This is totally grape!" Zack cried.

As the boys were busy eating, Drake thought of an idea.

"Does anyone want to play a round of big planet-collector?" Drake asked.

"Sure!" Zack said. "I love that game!"

"Yeah, me too," Seth agreed.

So the three boys each grabbed a set of controllers and turned on a large holographic screen.

"Watch out—go that way!" Seth directed.

Drake steered the video game spacecraft toward a planet, narrowly missing an asteroid blast.

"Now go left," Seth commanded.

Drake followed his directions, dodging asteroids and comets. After several rounds and many close calls, the boys made it to the end of the game. The trio happily gave one another a three-way high five.

"See, as long as you listen to me, we will always win!" Seth said.

Zack and Drake furrowed their brows at each other.

"Um, sure, Seth, we will listen to you—that is unless you tell us to jump into a volcano," Drake said. "Then you are on your own!"

Seth looked surprised for a moment, but then the three boys started to laugh. Seth laughed the loudest.

They glanced up as Ms. Rudolph came over to their seats. "We are going to be arriving on Digitron shortly. Make sure you buckle your seat belts for landing."

Zack fastened his seat belt. He couldn't believe they were almost there.

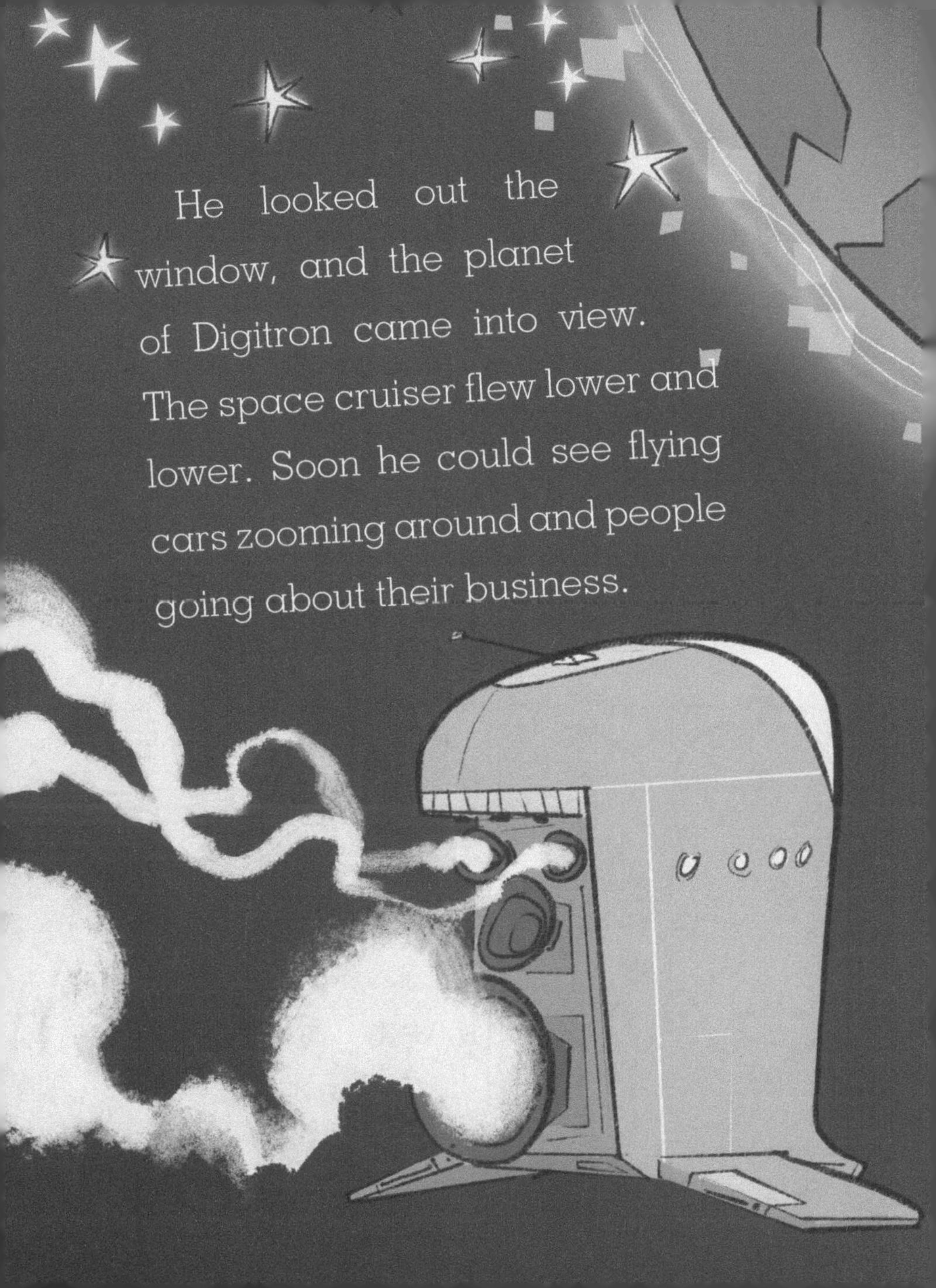

He looked out the window, and the planet of Digitron came into view. The space cruiser flew lower and lower. Soon he could see flying cars zooming around and people going about their business.

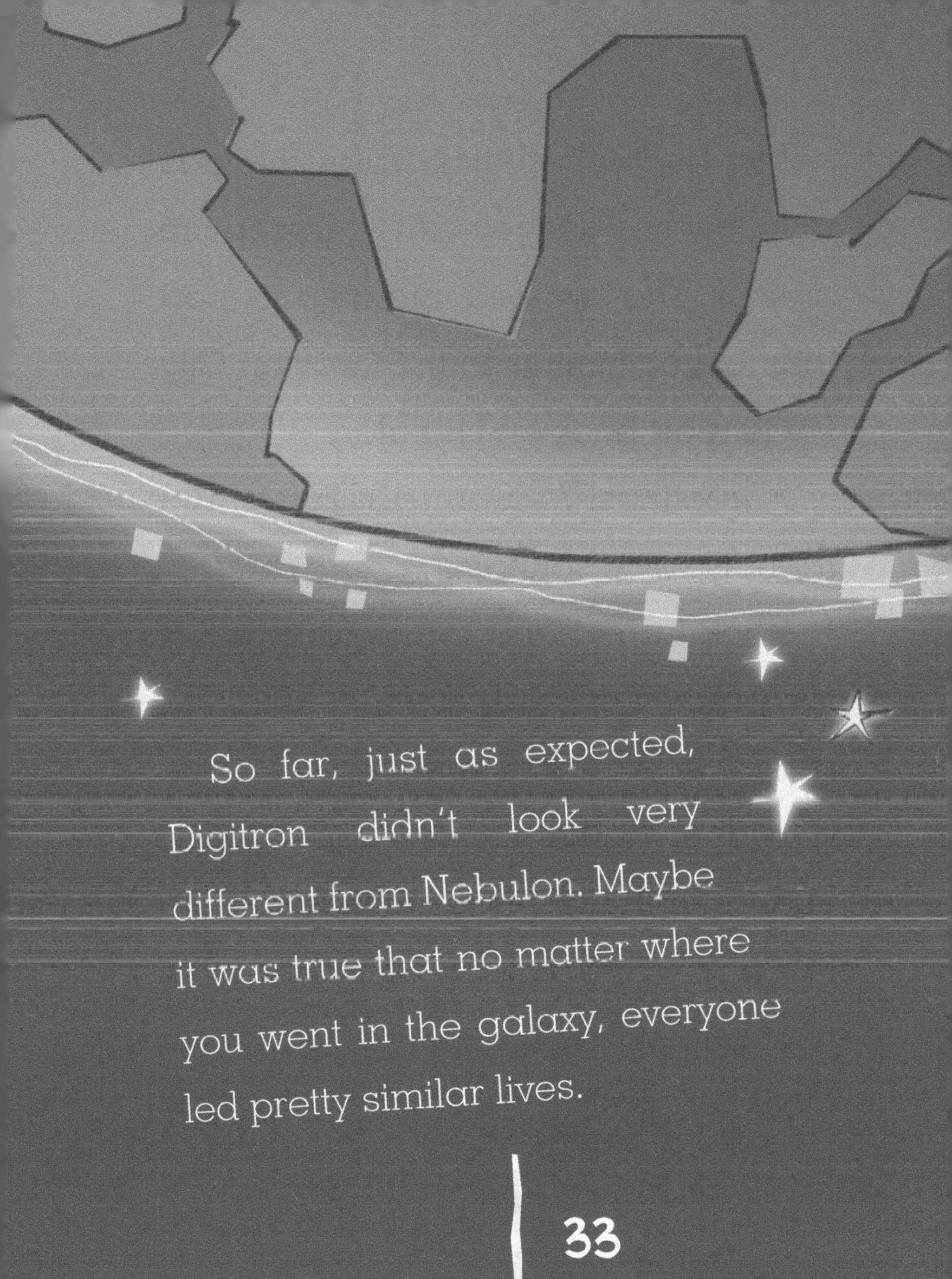

So far, just as expected, Digitron didn't look very different from Nebulon. Maybe it was true that no matter where you went in the galaxy, everyone led pretty similar lives.

Ms. Rudolph motioned for the kids to follow her as they exited the space cruiser. They walked into a spaceport that looked similar to the Creston City Spaceport back on Nebulon.

"Greetings! Welcome to Digitron!" a friendly voice sounded.

Zack turned and came face-to-face with a cube-shaped woman who looked just like a video game character. Her features were made up of small blocklike pixels.

"My name is Fiona Farkle. Welcome to our planet. I am here to take you to our special Digitron Virtual Gaming Dimension."

Zack and his friends looked at one another eagerly. They were about to be the first kids from Nebulon to ever step into a video game.

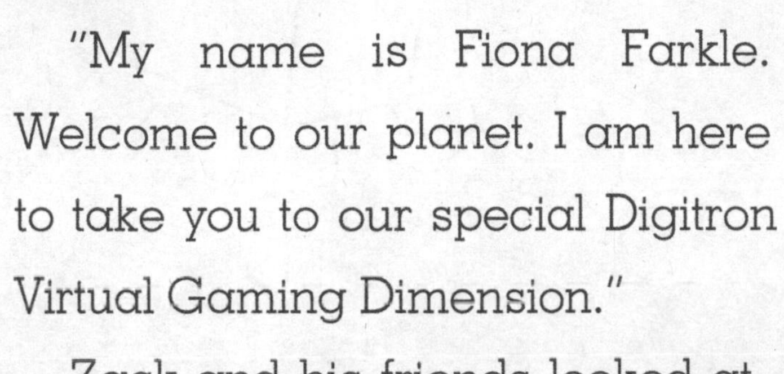

Chapter 4
The Gaming Portal

"First we need to head over to the shuttle, which will take us to the Virtual Gaming Portal. The portal connects the spaceport to Digitron's Virtual Gaming Dimension," Fiona explained. "It's the fastest way to access the gaming dimension."

Zack and the others followed her on board, and he stared out the window as the shuttle zoomed through the spaceport. The spaceport was built from floor to ceiling of glass, so Zack could see the world outside. From what he could tell, Digitron still looked similar to Nebulon.

The shuttle flew through a series of tunnels until it finally stopped at a landing port. After they exited the shuttle, Fiona turned to face Zack, Drake, and Seth.

"Here, these are for you," she said, handing each kid a device that looked similar to a hyperphone. "This will be your Virtual Gaming Assistant, or VGA, while you are in the Games. Keep them in your pockets at all times. The VGA is already loaded with your data, your full names, planets of origin, and, of course, your team name."

Zack looked at his vid-screen. It read:

ZACK NELSON. NEBULON. TEAM SPROCKETS.

Seth and Drake examined their vid-screens too.

"Ms. Rudolph, don't you get a Virtual Gaming Assistant too?" Zack asked.

"Oh no, I'm not participating in the games," Ms. Rudolph replied. "But I have a special badge here—see? It will allow me to watch you play."

"Yes, from here on out, the three of you will be on your own," Fiona added.

The kids then turned to Ms. Rudolph, suddenly getting a little nervous. "I know you will make Sprockets Academy and all of Nebulon proud!" she cried. "Good luck and have *fun*!"

Zack, Seth, and Drake waved goodbye, then turned to step into the elevator-like car Fiona said would take them through the portal.

"Remember, anything and everything that you least expect can happen in the Virtual Gaming Dimension," said Fiona. "Make sure to watch out for each other!" Then she waved goodbye.

"Wow, things are about to get real," Zack said, his voice filled with awe.

"Oh, don't worry. This is going to be a piece of cake," Seth said proudly.

As the doors closed, a panel on one of the walls lit up. Then strange symbols appeared, and the elevator began to zip smoothly through a dark tunnel. The kids could see flashing blue lights through the crack between the doors. A few minutes later, the elevator came to a stop. The doors opened, and Zack and his friends stepped outside.

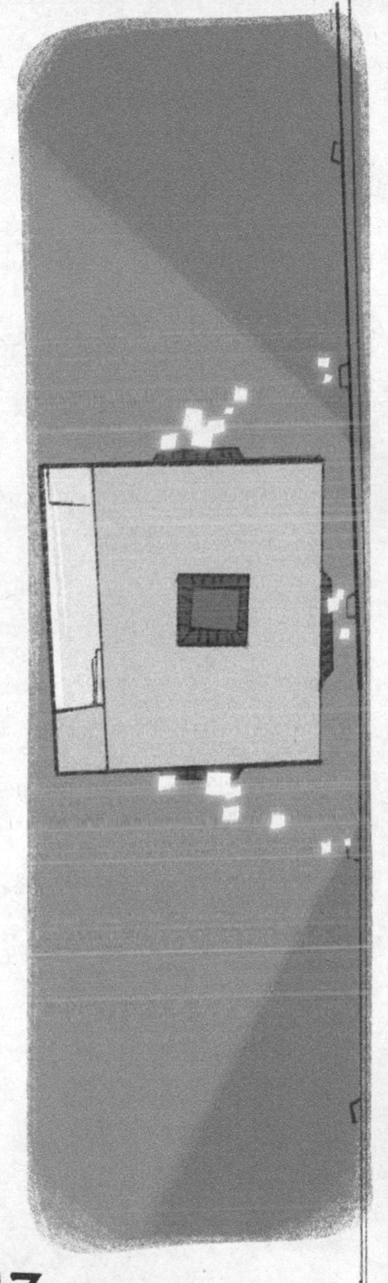

At once, all three friends gasped. The Virtual Gaming Dimension looked anything but ordinary—they were surrounded by towering mountains blanketed with tall, tall trees.

Chapter 5
Game Time!

As Zack and his friends moved away from the portal doors, they saw other kids standing in a clearing between the trees. *These must be our competitors,* Zack thought.

There were players from planets all across the galaxy.

Zack spotted people from Plexus and Araxie and Cisnos and many other places.

Zack looked around and spied a short, cube-shaped boy who was talking loudly with some other cube-shaped kids. Someone called him Zander. Zack guessed Zander's team must be from Digitron and wondered if being from this planet made them extra-good players.

Suddenly, a loud gong sound blasted through the air, and a voice echoed through the trees.

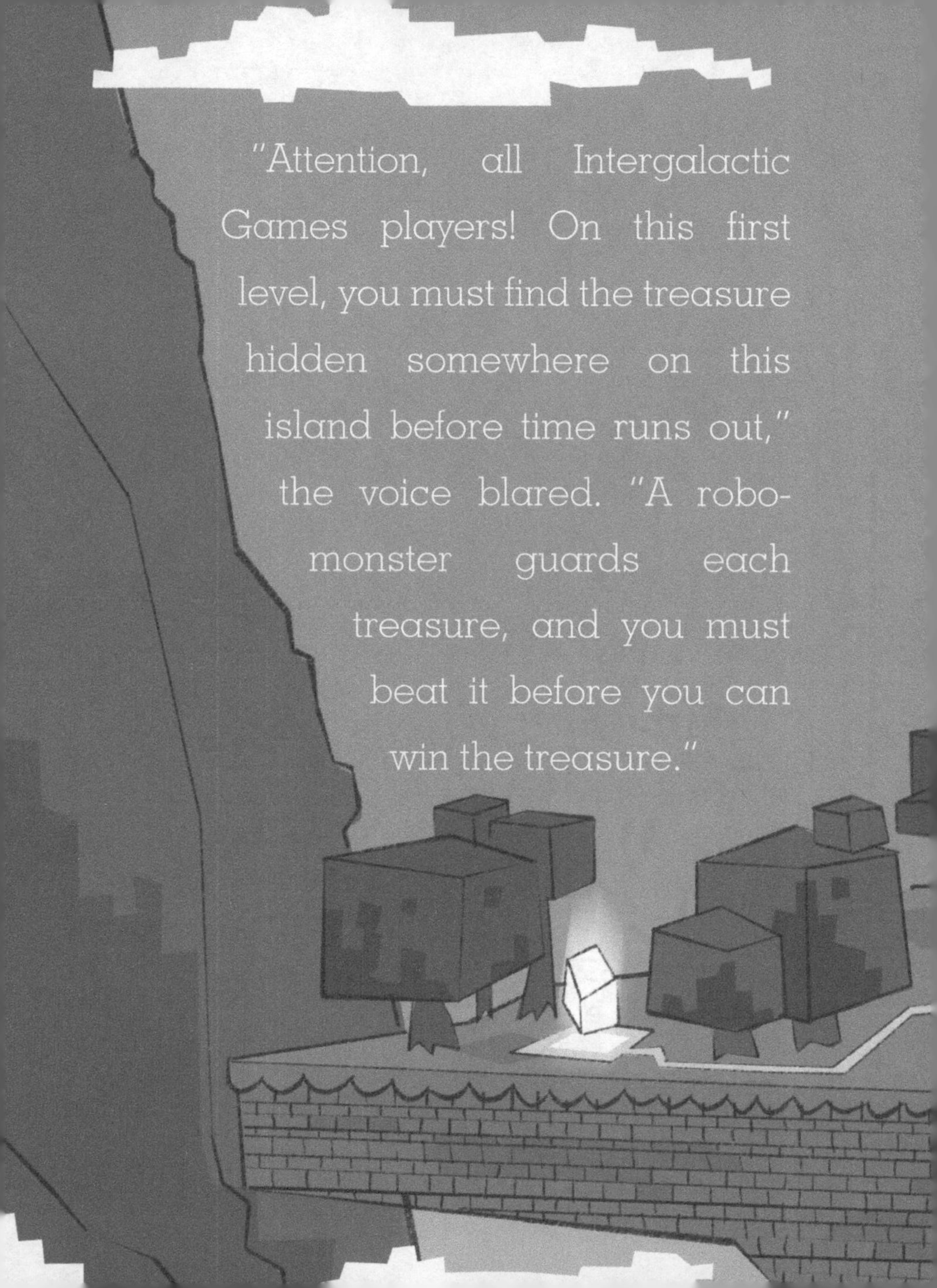

"Attention, all Intergalactic Games players! On this first level, you must find the treasure hidden somewhere on this island before time runs out," the voice blared. "A robo-monster guards each treasure, and you must beat it before you can win the treasure."

Zack tried his best to take mental notes.

"As you defeat more robo-monsters, you earn points and unlock stronger weapons," the voice continued. "Remember to check your pockets—you never know what handy tools you might be carrying. And finally, if one team member falls, the entire team loses the round."

A giant clock appeared in the sky, and a countdown began. The first round of the Intergalactic Games had begun.

"Quick! Check your pockets! " Seth directed.

Seth, Zack, and Drake stuck their hands in their pockets, feeling for their VGAs. Their mouths fell open with surprise as they each pulled out their very own bow with laser arrows!

"This is so grape! I have always wanted one of these!" Drake cheered.

Zack let out a half-hearted laugh. Somehow, having the bow and arrow in his hands made him a little nervous. The trio slowly started walking toward the trees.

"Look!" Seth called. He pointed ahead to a creature behind a giant tree. It had eight eyes, three arms, and was very hairy . . . for a robot.

"It's a monster! We have to get it!" Zack said. He held up his bow, nocked an arrow in the string, and pulled it back. He aimed, then let go.

The laser arrow whizzed through the air and struck the robo-monster. The boys watched as the robo-monster said, "Good shot! You win!"

"Whoa, we won!" Zack cried as his nerves instantly went away too.

"Hey, look! You scored a hundred and fifty points!" Drake exclaimed, pointing at the numbers that flashed in front of them.

"Cool! But we have to keep moving. There are more of those robo-monsters coming!" Zack called.

He and Drake each nocked an arrow and let it fly. Drake hit his robo-monster and watched as his points flashed in the air.

He and Drake kept shooting arrows, hitting target after target until there was a pause. Zack and Drake watched as the bows they had been holding flickered. Fortunately, the robo-monsters paused too.

Drake patted his pocket and fished out a sword. "Hey, look, I got upgraded!"

Zack felt inside his pocket. "No way, that's grape!"

The two friends gave each other a high five, but then realized that Seth was nowhere to be seen. The boys ran around until they found Seth hiding behind a rock.

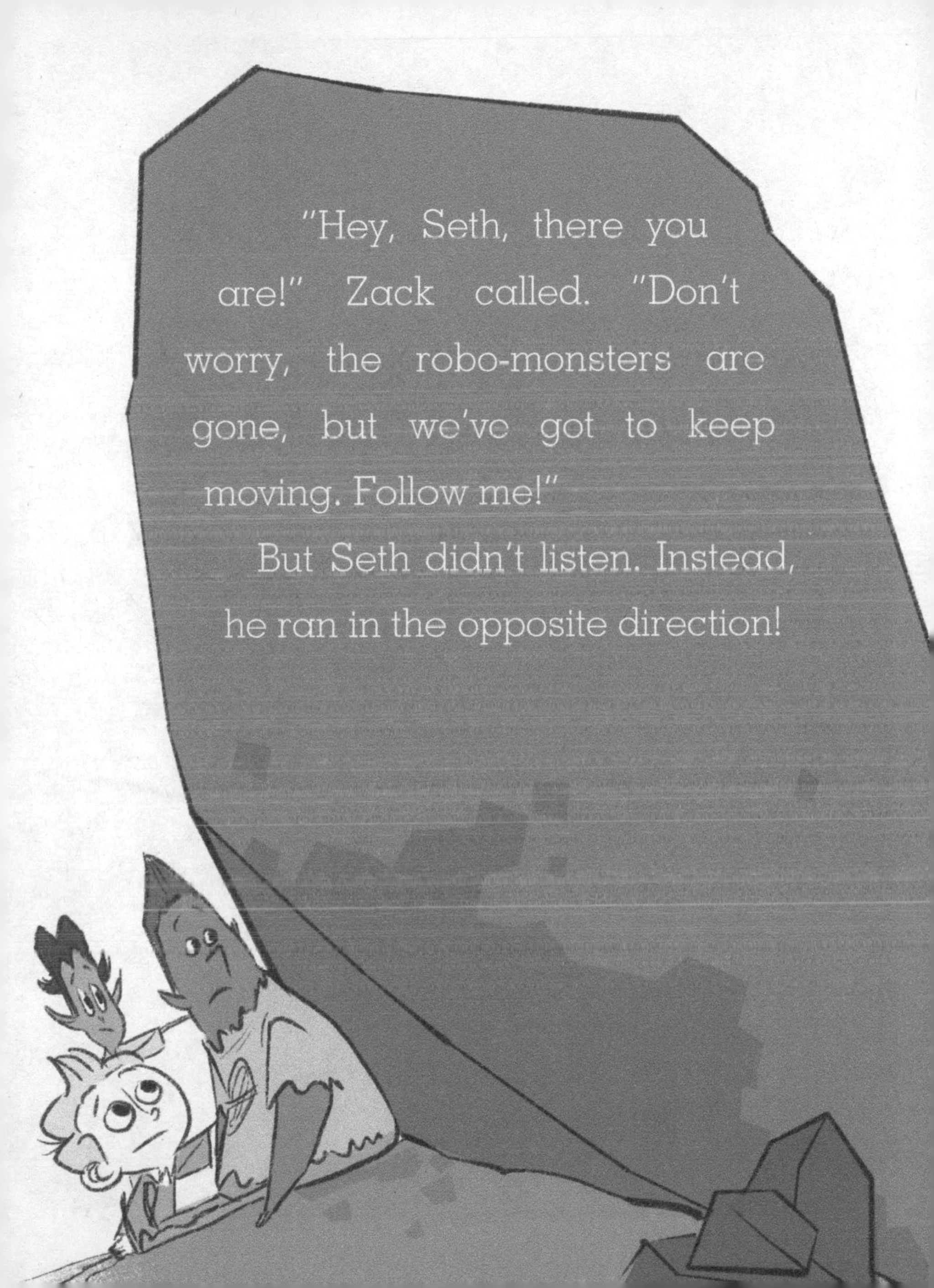

"Hey, Seth, there you are!" Zack called. "Don't worry, the robo-monsters are gone, but we've got to keep moving. Follow me!"

But Seth didn't listen. Instead, he ran in the opposite direction!

"Where are you going, Seth?"
Drake yelled.

Seth kept
running away, until,
suddenly . . . he vanished!

Drake and Zack ran to the spot where Seth had been standing. There was a floating window in the air. When Zack peered through it, he saw Seth and Zander, the Digitronian boy he'd noticed before, facing a vast hole. On the other side was a huge robo-monster guarding a pile of treasure.

Zander took aim at the monster with his bow and arrow. But as he released the arrow, he lost his balance and pushed Seth off the edge!

"NOOOOOO!" the boys yelled at the top of their lungs as they watched their friend disappear down the hole.

Chapter 6
The Race Begins!

"Oh no! We have to help him!" Zack cried. He and Drake jumped through the flickering window, then stared down at the hole Seth had fallen into. It really looked like a volcano!

Zack remembered the joke Drake had made on the space cruiser.

It had been about not following Seth into a volcano. "This doesn't count as a volcano, does it?" he asked. "It's just a game—right?"

Drake shrugged. The two friends closed their eyes tight and jumped.

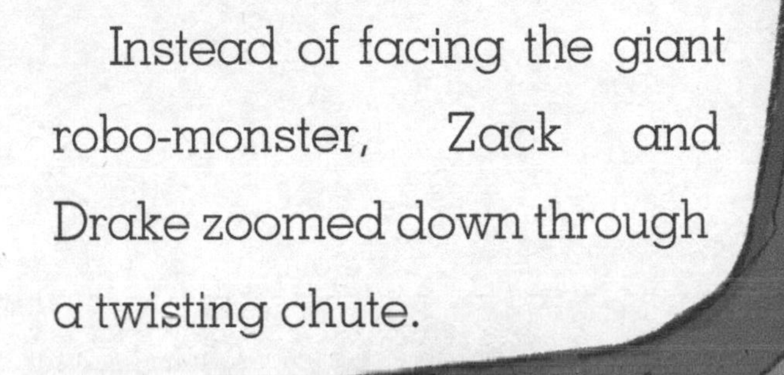

Instead of facing the giant robo-monster, Zack and Drake zoomed down through a twisting chute.

And soon the slide spat them onto their feet. Zack and Drake looked around. Their surroundings had changed into a giant racecourse. They had reached the next level of the game!

Another gong sounded, and the announcer said, "Attention, Intergalactic Games players. On this second level, each team member will participate in a kart race. There is one round with five laps. Good gaming to all!"

Zack glanced around, hoping to find Seth, but he spotted the leaderboard first. The Sprockets were at the very bottom, with zero points.

"Oh no," he groaned.

Digitron was at the top. Zander must have captured the treasure after he and Drake followed Seth into the hole.

"The Digitronians are winning," Drake said. "Do you think Zander made Seth fall into the hole on purpose?"

"Not sure, but that's certainly what it looked like," Zack answered with a frustrated sigh.

That's when Seth came over with an embarrassed look on his face. "Hi, guys. I did not know we would lose all our points because I fell."

Zack shook his head and welcomed his friend back with a big smile. He didn't want Seth to feel any pressure about what another player did.

"Don't worry, we can still win this level," he said. "The game isn't over yet!"

Then they walked over to a parking lot filled with racing vehicles. Zack chose one that looked like a rocket ship. Drake's racer looked like a flying submarine, and Seth picked one that looked like a monster truck.

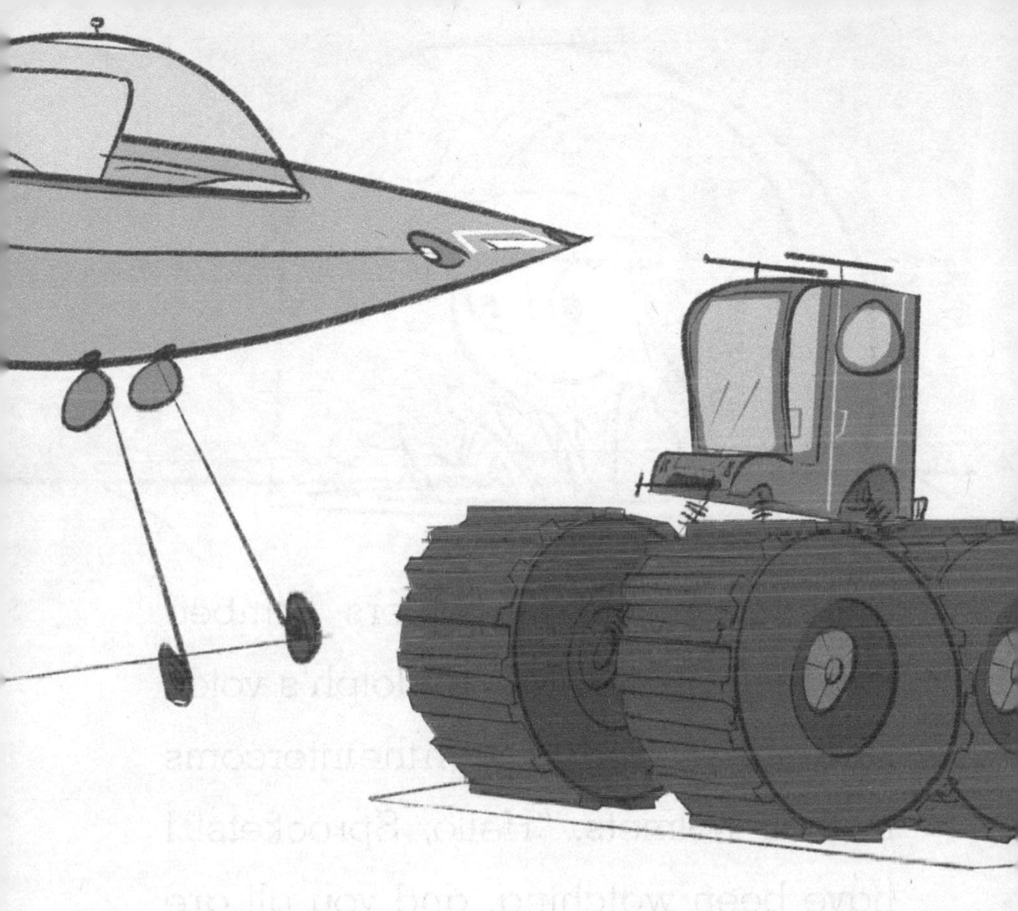

"Hey! Do not forget to wear your helmets," Drake reminded his friends. Safety was always most important.

As Zack and the others climbed into their racers, Ms. Rudolph's voice suddenly buzzed through the intercoms in their helmets. "Hello, Sprockets! I have been watching, and you all are doing great. Remember, stay focused, and watch out for one another! And as they say on Digitron, good gaming to all!"

She clicked off, and then another giant sign appeared. As soon as it said GO! they were off and the race was on!

Chapter 7

Crash and Berry Burnout!

Quickly, Zack steered his rocket race car to the front of the line of racers, just as an orange-haired Cisnosian was closing in on him.

As Zack peeled around the track, he noticed that there were blinking treasure boxes on the roadway.

He guided his car to one, and the vid-screen display in his dashboard flashed: **CHOCOBERRY SAUCE.**

"I wonder what that does," Zack said to himself.

He pressed the button, and a stream of thick, brown sludge poured from the back of his car, and covered the ship behind him. As soon as the racer drove through it, their ship skidded, then slowed to a stop.

"Yipee-wah-wah!" cheered Zack. Then he looked in his rearview monitor.

Seth had avoided the mess and was close behind in second place. The Digitronian kid named Zander was in third place. Zack didn't see Drake, so he checked his virtual map on the dash. Drake was trailing near the back of the pack.

Zack sped around the track twice, swiftly taking turns and scooping up treasure prizes along the way. He kept his lead, but on the latest turn, Zander overtook Seth for second place. No matter how hard Zack pushed, he could not shake Zander.

Just as Zack came to another bend in the track, he reached the spot where he had spilled the Chocoberry sauce. It was too late to get out of the way.

Before Zack knew it, the rocket ship race car spun sideways, then slowed to a crawl as the sauce clung to his wheels. Zander, who had been right on Zack's tail, also slid out of control and smashed into Zack's car.

Zack watched helplessly as Seth and the rest of Zander's team finished the race.

Zack had lost the race for the Sprockets. Now they wouldn't get any points again.

Chapter 8

Game Over, Nebulon?

"If you had not used Chocoberry sauce and crashed, we could have won this round," Seth said to Zack, his voice filled with frustration.

The players were in the area beyond the finish line, waiting for the next level and their new instructions.

"Well, if you had listened to me when we were fighting the robo-monsters, we might have won that round!" Zack told Seth. "And anyway, Drake was at the back of the pack."

As the words came out of his mouth, Zack felt a pit settle in his belly. The Games were not turning out to be all that fun, and now he and his friends were fighting.

Zack kicked his sludgy ship with a splat of disappointment. Would competing in the Intergalactic Games ruin everything?

The three friends stood with their backs to one another.

Ms. Rudolph made her way to where the players waited. "Team Sprockets, the Intergalactic Games have strict rules about good sportsmanship," she said. "Remember, arguing won't solve your problem. You've got to find a way to help one another."

Zack pondered this, and he looked at his friends. It was clear that Ms. Rudolph's warning had stirred them, too.

"Sorry, guys, I do not think we should fight," Drake said. "We came here to compete against the other teams, not one another!"

"You're right, Drake. I agree," Zack said.

"So do I," Seth chimed in. "Even if we do not win, we can still enjoy ourselves."

"That's right," Zack added. "I'm really sorry that I wasn't nice before."

"I am sorry, too," Seth said. "I should not have blamed you for losing the race."

"Now is the time to make a plan to win!" Drake cried.

The friends huddled together and began to plot. As they talked, Zander wandered over.

The Sprockets looked at him, confused. What could Zander possibly want?

"Greetings, Nebulites. I have a special proposal for you."

"What is it?" Seth asked.

"My team and I think Digitron and Nebulon should combine forces for this last round," Zander said.

Right then, Zack's mouth hit the floor. *Could Zander be serious?* Zack wondered. He was pretty sure that Zander had not played fair on the first two levels. He had pushed Seth off the cliff and then crashed into Zack's car, after all.

"I am not so sure," Zack said. "Why should we trust you after everything that has happened?"

"I know that you might think I knocked Seth into the hole. But I did not do it on purpose—I was trying to protect him from the robo-monster, but then I tripped."

"What about the car crash?" Zack asked.

"I tried to get out of your way so you would have room to avoid the Chocoberry sauce," Zander said.

Zack couldn't believe it.

Had this all been a major misunderstanding this whole time?

"I think we could work well as a team," Zander continued. He lifted his palm out for a Nebulon handshake. Zack, Drake, and Seth did the same.

Zack wasn't sure about joining forces. But with the team being down so many points, Seth and Drake convinced him that they had nothing to lose. If they were going to make a comeback, they'd need all hands on deck.

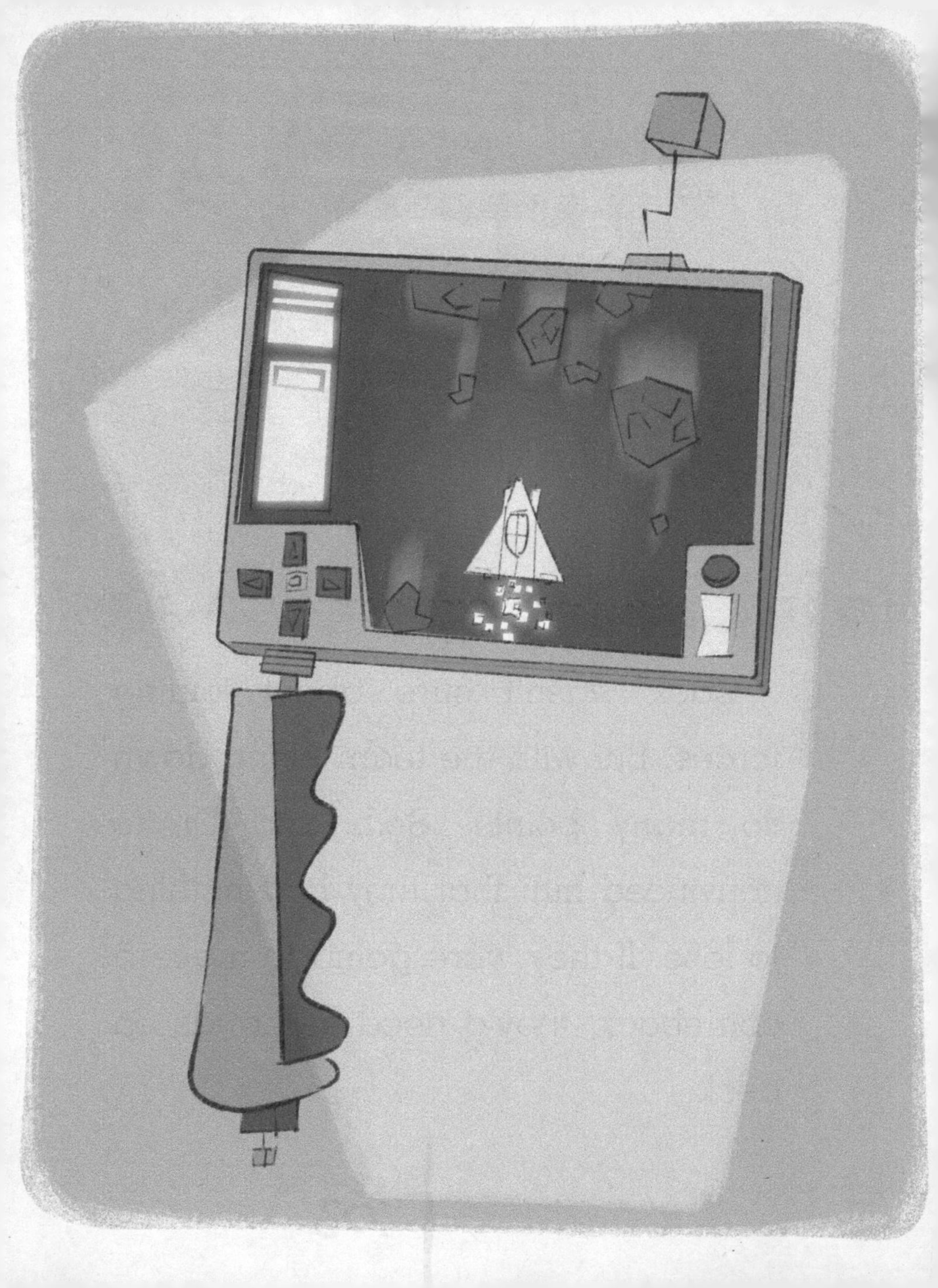

Chapter 9
Asteroid Blast!

"Attention, all Intergalactic Games players. This third and final level will be a live round of Asteroid Blast, which those of you from Nebulon may know. It was recently developed for Digitron, and this marks the first time it will be played here. Good gaming to all."

Zack and his friends smiled in surprise.

"Yippee-wah-wah!" Drake shouted. "We have played so much Asteroid Blast on our hyperphones, there is no way we can lose this round!"

Zander's teammates came over, and Zander introduced them to the Sprockets. "Drake and Zack and Seth are from Nebulon. We have agreed to team up and help one another out," Zander explained.

"If you are from Nebulon, you must be super good at playing Asteroid Blast," one of the Digitronians said.

"We know how to play it on our hyperphones, but we have never played *inside* the game," Zack said.

"Your experience will definitely be a help," Zander said. "We will watch out for you, and you will watch out for us."

"You got it! It's a deal!" Zack said.

Each of the teams was given a new spaceship. Before the Sprockets boarded theirs, Seth reminded everyone of the rules.

"There should be three blasters on board, so we each have to zap asteroids on our own side of the ship. And remember, we can rack up triple points if we zap fast!"

"Yes, Seth is right—blast quickly," Drake said, smiling. "And watch out for asteroids coming toward both our ships!"

"We are on it!" Zack shouted with a grin. "If we all stay focused, both our teams have a shot at winning a trophy."

Everyone boarded their ships and found their blasters.

With almost perfect aim, Seth, Drake, and Zack blasted away at the fast-flying asteroids.

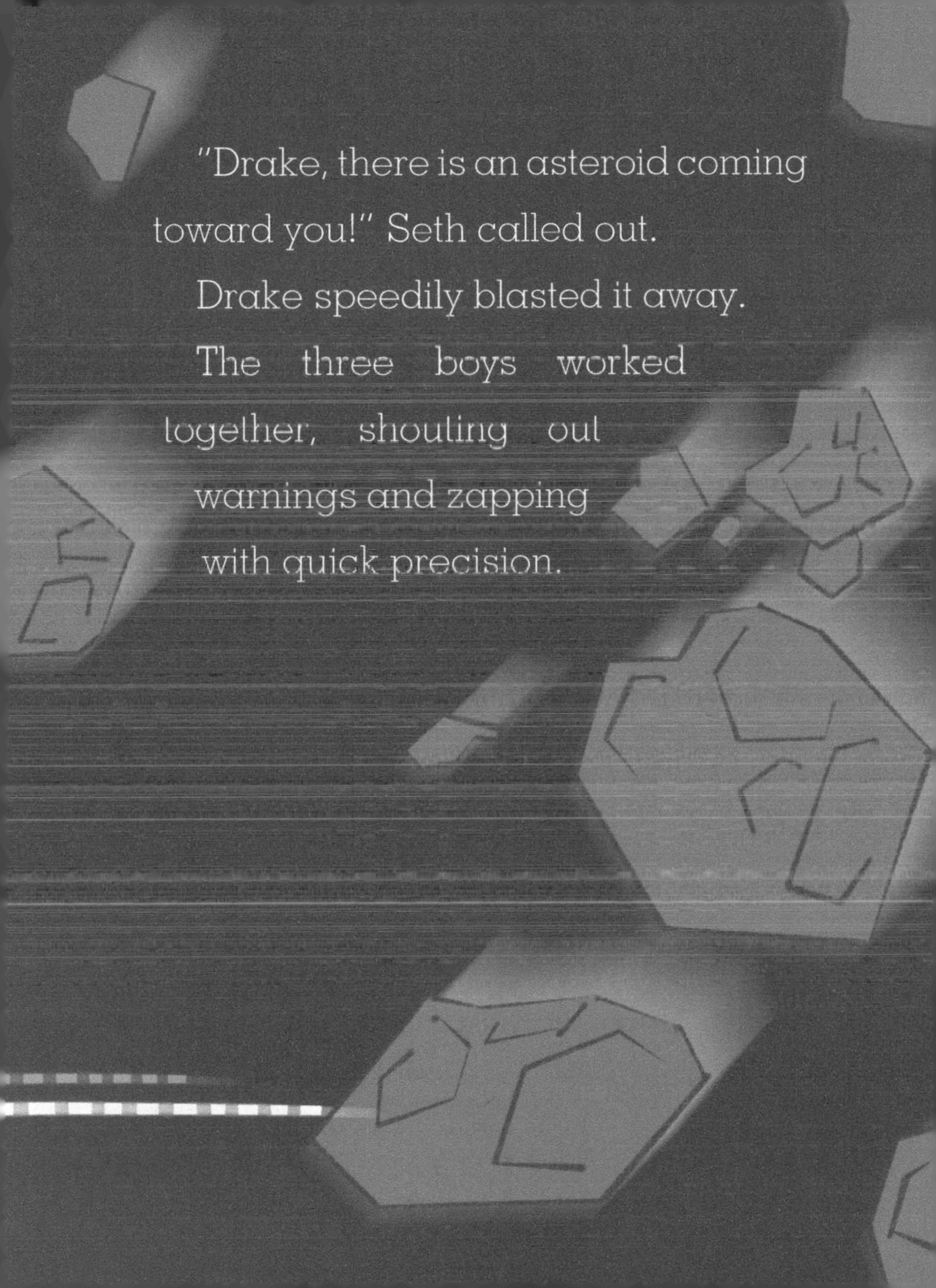

"Drake, there is an asteroid coming toward you!" Seth called out.

Drake speedily blasted it away.

The three boys worked together, shouting out warnings and zapping with quick precision.

Suddenly, Zack noticed a large asteroid headed for Zander's ship.

"Zander, look out. There is an asteroid headed your way!" Zack messaged.

The Digitronians quickly turned their ship and blasted the asteroid.

"Thanks, Zack!" Zander messaged back.

"Sure thing!" Zack said. "And look out again. Here comes another one!"

Soon the Sprockets had racked up so many points, they had climbed to the very top of the leaderboard, and the Digitronians were right behind them in second place.

When the timer clock counted down to zero, Zack, Seth, and Drake high-fived. Working as a team felt great, and it made winning even better.

Chapter 10
Leaderboard Comebacks

"I can't believe the Intergalactic Games are already over," Zack whispered to Drake as they waited for the award ceremony to begin.

They watched as Fiona Farkle came out onto a small stage and waved to the audience.

"Good evening, players and spectators. This year's Intergalactic Games were a great success and Digitron has been honored to host you all," she said with a smile. "Now it is time to award the top three teams. In third place is Nebulon!"

The Sprockets hooted and high-fived as they made their way up to the podium.

"I cannot believe that after everything, we are up here!" Drake said, beaming at his friends.

"This is the grapest!" Zack said as Fiona handed him a sparkling trophy. He imagined bringing it home to show their family and friends.

"In second place is my home planet, Digitron," Fiona announced.

Zack, Drake, and Seth smiled and cheered loudly for Zander and their new Digitronian friends.

"And in first place is Ciscos. Congratulations to all!"

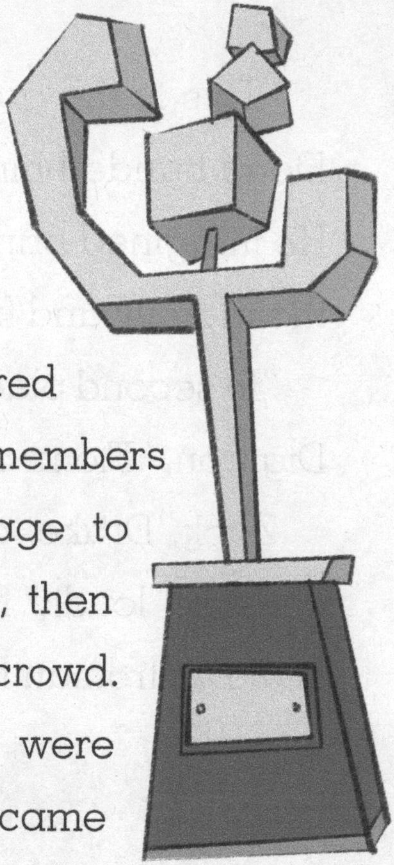

The orange-haired Cisnosian team members came up to the stage to receive their awards, then turned to smile at the crowd.

After the awards were given out, Zander came over to Zack and his friends. "Thank you for everything, Nebulites. We would never have gotten back on the leaderboard without your help. We hope you will come visit again—but next time, just for fun," he added. "Real life is just as fun as—and *way* more normal than—the Gaming Dimension."

"We would love that!" Zack cried happily.

With that, Ms. Rudolph led the Nebulon gang back through the Virtual Gaming Portal to the Digitron Spaceport to begin the trip home.

As their space cruiser left from Digitron, Zack watched as it became a tiny dot in the sky and thought about all the cool things he had to tell his family when he got home. He'd had the chance to live out one of his best dreams ever: being a real-life video game character.

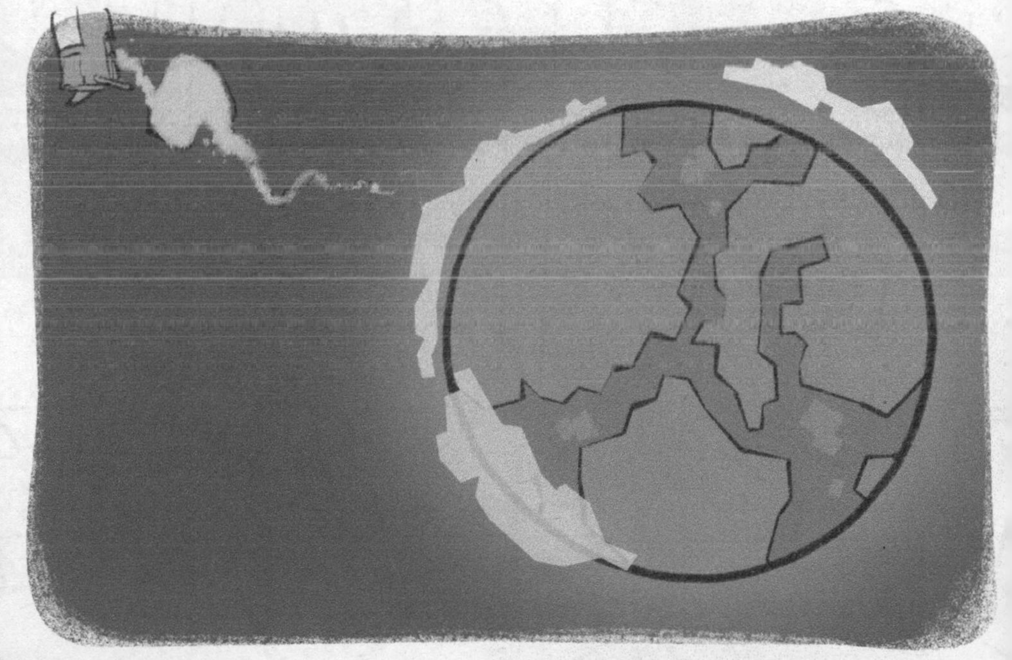

It had been a long day. Zack and his friends had gamed well and played hard.

"I'm happy we're going home," Zack said, looking over at his teammates. "Even if we don't battle robo-monsters or race through racetracks or blast asteroids in real life on Nebulon, when we're together, any adventure is really out of this world!"

HERE ARE SOME MORE OUT-OF-THIS-WORLD

GALAXY ZACK

ADVENTURES!

CPSIA information can be obtained
at www.ICGtesting.com
Printed in the USA
BVHW080256171122
652006BV00016B/80

9 781665 919258